To Kalina! Tynan~

Happy reading!

Celeste

MAddr

Maddy
and the
Magic Penny

Written by Celeste Scheinberg

Illustrated by Angela Zhu

Maddy and the Magic Penny

Text written by Celeste Scheinberg

Illustrated by Angela Zhu

Published by
Conmad Books
222 W. Pueblo Street
Santa Barbara, California 93101
805-689-5065

Edited by Gail Kearns
Design and Art Direction by Penelope C. Paine
Typography by Cirrus Design

ISBN-13: 978-0-9788402-0-4
ISBN-10: 0-9788402-0-8

Printed in China

In memory of Francisco (a.k.a. Paquito), who was loved by many. He was an avid reader, and he will be in our hearts and thoughts always.

Thank you to my family:
My husband, Rick, a great husband, father, and doctor
My kids, Conor and Maddy
My mom, Marilyn Kelly Turbeville

When she went to pick up Maddy from school, her mom knew something was wrong. Maddy did not speak the whole way home.

As soon as they got home, Maddy ran into the kitchen, sat on the stool at the counter, and rested her chin in her hands. "I had a bad day," Maddy said with a big sigh.

"What happened?" her mom asked as she handed Maddy a glass of chocolate milk.

"First," said Maddy, "No one would give me a turn on the swings, not even Alexandra!"

"Then the boys laughed at me because I was wearing this dress. They said it was for babies." Maddy pointed to her dress with the giraffe on the front. It was one of her favorite birthday presents from her grandma.

"Is that so," her mom nodded, sitting down next to her.

"Yes," Maddy answered glumly, "and then I had no one to eat lunch with because Emma was not at school and I had to sit all alone."

"That sounds terrible," Maddy's mom said as she gave her a big hug. "Maybe tomorrow will be a better day."

"Oh, Mommy, I wish you could go to school with me. You are my best friend." Maddy said.

"Well, Maddy, I would if I could but grownups aren't allowed to go to school with their children," her mom replied.

"Well, then, I wish you could be little for a day just like me. Then you could come with me, right?"

The next day Maddy still felt upset. She wasn't sure she wanted to go to school. "Maddy, it's time to go," her mom called out, opening the car door for her.

When they arrived at school and Maddy got out of the car, something caught her eye.

It was a penny. It wasn't just shiny like the new pennies Maddy had seen before; this one sparkled.

"Look, Mom, a penny!" Maddy exclaimed as she picked up the coin off the wet ground.

Maddy closed her eyes and made a wish.

When she opened them up, her mom was a little girl!

They stared at each other, totally surprised.

Mrs. Smith, Maddy's favorite teacher, came up to them. "What are you girls doing out here in the parking lot without your mommies?" she asked. "Quickly, come along to your classroom."

What could Maddy and her mom say? Who would believe them?

When they were inside the gate, Maddy told her mom what she had wished on the penny. "It must be a magic penny!" Maddy's mom whispered. "You only wished me to be little for a day, right?"

"Yes, Mom, only for a day," Maddy answered, laughing. They skipped to class, hand in hand.

In class, Maddy and her mom made beautiful watercolor
rainbows.

Then they played dolls with the other girls.

"This is my cousin visiting for the day," Maddy said. She didn't want to tell them it was really her mom.

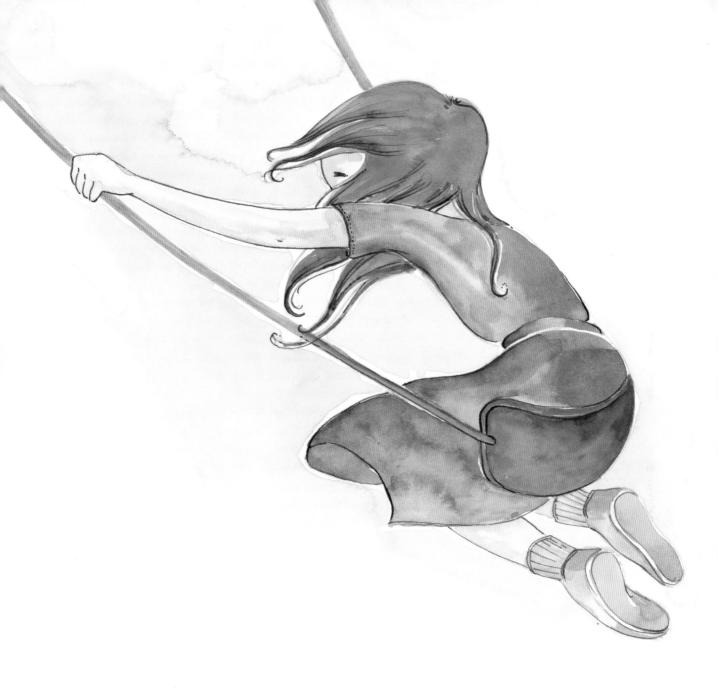

"Let's see if we can get a turn on the swings," Maddy said to her mom. As usual, the swings were all taken, so the girls waited and waited. Maddy's mom finally asked, "Can we have a turn please?" "Okay," the other children replied.

After their turn on the swings, Maddy and her mom went over to the jungle gym. Two of the boys started to tease Maddy.

"It's not nice to tease people," Maddy's mom scolded them. "Do you want to play with us?" "No way," they answered and quickly ran off to play with the other boys.

Because Maddy's mom didn't know that she would magically turn into a little girl, she didn't bring anything to eat for lunch. Maddy shared her peanut butter and jelly sandwich, "Thank you," her mom said. "Yummy, my favorite."

Then they noticed that one of the boys who had teased Maddy was sitting alone. "Do you want to eat lunch with us?" Maddy's mom asked. The boy smiled and came over to sit with them.

Later the class read a story about squirrels and sang a song. Maddy's mom was embarrassed because she didn't know the words. "It's okay," Maddy said. "Mommies don't have to know everything."

When it was time to go home, Maddy and her mom walked to the parking lot. "Quick, Maddy," her mom said. "Wish me back into a big person so we can go home."

For a moment Maddy panicked. What if she couldn't wish her mom back into a big person? Who would take care of her?

She took the magic penny out of her pocket, held it tight, and closed her eyes.

21

When Maddy opened her eyes, she wasn't at school at all; she was still in her bed. It had all been a dream!

Her mom came into the room and she was still a grown up.

"Are you ready for school Maddy?" her mom asked, pulling back her covers. "It's a lovely sunny day!"

Maddy looked over and saw the sparkling
penny on her nightstand. "Yes, Mom,
I am. And you don't have to be
little to be my best friend. I like
you just the way you are."